Fading friendships

Now that she was aware of all the other changes, Grace was noticing that the gang spent less time together at school. They all still sat together at lunchtime, but often Kester and Raj went off to play soccer with Julio and Jason, and now they didn't usually ask the girls to join them.

Grace and Maria were quite good at soccer, though Crishell had never played with them much. But during all the wedding conversations, they'd gotten out of the habit of playing with the boys. Grace realized that she was more often in a group of girls now, with Crishell and Maria and often La Tasha and Sophie as well, while Kester and Raj spent time with other boys. The gang still came around to Grace's on the weekend, but now she wondered how long that would last.

OTHER BOOKS YOU MAY ENJOY

Bravo, Grace!

Mary Hoffman
Illustrations by June Allan

PUFFIN BOOKS
An Imprint of Penguin Group (USA) Inc.

For Janetta

PUFFIN BOOKS
Published by the Penguin Group
Penguin Young Readers Group, 345 Hudson Street, New York, New York 10014, U.S.A.
Penguin Group (Canada), 90 Eglinton Avenue East, Suite 700, Toronto, Ontario, Canada M4P 2Y3
(a division of Pearson Penguin Canada Inc.)
Penguin Books Ltd, 80 Strand, London WC2R 0RL, England
Penguin Ireland, 25 St Stephen's Green, Dublin 2, Ireland (a division of Penguin Books Ltd)
Penguin Group (Australia), 250 Camberwell Road, Camberwell, Victoria 3124, Australia
(a division of Pearson Australia Group Pty Ltd)
Penguin Books India Pvt Ltd, 11 Community Centre,
Panchsheel Park, New Delhi - 110 017, India
Penguin Group (NZ), 67 Apollo Drive, Rosedale, Auckland 0632, New Zealand
(a division of Pearson New Zealand Ltd)
Penguin Books (South Africa) (Pty) Ltd, 24 Sturdee Avenue,
Rosebank, Johannesburg 2196, South Africa

Registered Offices: Penguin Books Ltd, 80 Strand, London WC2R 0RL, England

First published in Great Britain by Frances Lincoln Children's Books, 2005
Published by Puffin Books, a division of Penguin Young Readers Group, 2011

3 5 7 9 10 8 6 4 2

Bravo, Grace! copyright © Frances Lincoln Limited, 2005
Text copyright © Mary Hoffman, 2005
Illustrations copyright © June Allan, 2005

CIP DATA IS AVAILABLE

Puffin Books ISBN 978-0-14-241850-5

Set in Goudy Old Style

Printed in the United States of America

Contents

Grace is a girl who loves stories. The first story about her was Amazing Grace, where she learned from her nana that she could be and do anything she wanted. Stories often help Grace to decide what to do and be, though sometimes the traditional ones confuse her, as in Grace and Family, where she decided to write her own story to make her feel better about her father's new family in The Gambia. That helped her to accept Jatou, her stepmother, and her half siblings, Neneh and Bakary.

Grace returned in two storybooks of her own—Starring Grace and Encore, Grace!—in which her life with her friends and family began to change. Now here are nine more stories about Grace's gang, the changing friendships, her ma's marriage to Vincent, their new living arrangements, and in some ways the biggest change of all. And, of course, there are stories involving stories. . . .

Grace Goes Through the Gate

⸙

"How can a room as small as mine have so much stuff in it?" demanded Grace.

It was the busiest New Year that she had ever known. Normally, just starting a new school term without her best friend Aimee would have been huge enough, but now…

"I thought we had plenty of changes last year," she told Nana, as they went through Grace's things, "but this is the biggest change of all."

"Don't worry about it, honey," said Nana. "You'll soon settle down to your new routine when we've got everything sorted out at the house."

But Grace wasn't really worried; it was all pretty exciting. They were getting organized to move. At least, Grace and Ma were. Nana was staying put. If anyone had told Grace a year ago that she and Ma would move out of their garden apartment, leaving Nana behind, she would never have believed them. For as long as Grace could remember, they had all lived together in that apartment.

"It wasn't always this way," Ma tried to explain. "When we lived here with your papa, Nana wasn't with us. She moved in after Grandpa died and your papa went away."

Grace couldn't remember any of that and she couldn't remember Grandpa either. She couldn't remember the Papa of those days, who was married to Ma but moved out when Grace was still little. But she knew the Papa of now, because she had visited him in The Gambia with his new family: his wife, Jatou, and their children, Neneh and Bakary. Now, they wrote to each other every month and spoke on the phone once a week. It wasn't as good as having him around all the time, but it was better than knowing him just from old photos.

Grace's ma was getting married again and her new husband, Vincent, would be moving in with them. The little apartment would have been bursting at the seams if Nana hadn't come up with a solution. The house that Ma and Grace and Vince were moving into was really Nana's and it was just over the garden fence from the apartment. It used to belong to Grace's old friend, Mrs. Myerson, who had died that winter and left it to Nana.

"It was a surprise to me when Gerda's lawyer told me about the house," Nana said. "I never dreamed I'd own a house of my own—let alone at my age."

"But you were very kind to Mrs. Myerson," said Grace. Secretly, she wondered what it would be like moving in there. The house was dark and had bars on all the windows. When Grace and her friends first visited it, they thought it must be haunted. But both Ma and Nana told her it would be all right.

"Mrs. Myerson had no family left," said Ma, coming in with a pile of ironing. She sat down on Grace's bed. "I think Nana and you and your friends were like a family to her those last few months."

Since Christmas, when Vince had asked Ma to marry him and Nana had told them about Mrs. Myerson's house, they had talked about it a lot.

"Just think, Grace," Nana often said. "You can have two bedrooms, one here and one there. And whenever you want, you can come and spend the night here, just like before."

Grace liked that idea. She had a very tiny bedroom in the apartment and now she could have a much bigger one and choose exactly how to decorate it.

"We will only be just across the garden from Nana," said Ma, smoothing Grace's newly ironed bedsheets. "You'll still see her every day."

Grace heard the sound of a key in the door and knew that meant Vince had arrived. Ma smiled and jumped up, leaving the ironing in an untidy heap. Grace and Nana exchanged looks; they couldn't remember seeing Ma so happy.

When they went downstairs, they found Vince sitting on the sofa drinking coffee with Ma. He was dressed in jeans and a checkered shirt and had brought a toolbox with him. Propped up against the sofa was a large wooden gate.

Grace's eyes widened. "What's that for?" she asked.

"It's your magic gateway," said Vince, winking. "It will let you slip between your old and new lives in seconds."

Grace liked the sound of that. She went out into the garden with the grown-ups to watch Vince work. "You can help, if you like, Grace," he said. "I'll need someone to hand me screws and things."

By the time Grace's friends arrived, the gate was finished and where there had been a high fence to scramble over, there was now just a latch and a push between the two gardens.

"Wow!" said Maria. "You'll be able to get from one home to another so easily. I have to cross town on two buses to see my dad."

"But that's because your parents are divorced," said Crishell. "Like mine. They don't want to live close together, like Grace's family."

"I bet my ma and papa live further apart than any other divorced parents," said Grace. "They live on different continents, not just different streets."

"Who's talking about divorce?" said Nana, coming out with a tray of warm shortbread she had just made. "Grace's ma is getting married and that's what this gate is all about—keeping the family together, not breaking it apart."

"I'm not sure I like it as much as climbing over the fence to Mrs. Myerson's," said Kester, his mouth full of shortbread. "That made it more of an adventure."

"Well, adventure or not," said Vince, "I can tell you it's going to make life a lot easier coming and going while we get the old house fixed up."

He ceremoniously opened the new gate and showed them all through. Nana led the way, with a bunch of keys. They all walked across the grass, followed by Paw-Paw the cat, to the back door of their old friend's house.

Nana unlocked it and pulled it open, letting the pale winter sunlight in. The house had a sad and quiet feeling and it was hard for Grace to imagine living there.

"Do you think it will ever feel like home?" she whispered to Nana.

" 'Course it will," said Vince. "Just you wait till we've fixed it up. And remember, you've already chosen your room on the second floor.

Imagine actually climbing stairs up to bed—you haven't done that before, have you?"

That made Grace think of all the games she could play, using the stairs as steps in a tower, or ladders up walls, or pirate-ship rigging.

One of today's jobs was going to be getting the bars off all the windows and Kester and Maria were excited to help Vince do it. Ma and Nana were measuring for new curtains in all the rooms. Crishell and Raj were going to make a list of all Mrs. Myerson's furniture and Grace was going to decide what she wanted to do with her room.

She sat on the iron bed on the stiff, shiny blue bedspread that Nana called a "counterpane," with Paw-Paw on her lap, looking around the strange room. There was a dark wooden chest of drawers with a mirror in three sections on top of it and a large heavy wardrobe in the corner. The walls were a rather dirty pale blue-green and there were gray prints of old castles in Germany, which Grace rather liked. But she couldn't imagine this being her own bedroom. It was so grown-up.

There was a knock at the door and Raj and Crishell came in. Crishell had a very efficient-looking clipboard and was writing down all the furniture as Raj described it, and they had already finished downstairs. Now they looked round Grace's new room.

"More dark wood," said Raj. "It's a bit gloomy, isn't it?"

"It will look a lot lighter when the bars are off," said Crishell, seeing that Grace looked a bit worried. "And you can paint it bright colors too, can't you, Grace?"

Grace nodded. "I can choose. And I don't have to keep any of the furniture I don't want."

"I wonder what Mrs. Myerson used this room for," said Raj. The gang never used to come upstairs when they visited the old lady and they were a bit overwhelmed by the big bedrooms and their old-fashioned furniture. Vince and Grace's ma were going to have Mrs. Myerson's old room and there would still be two to spare—plenty of room for Nana to visit.

"Didn't she live on her own?" asked Crishell, who wasn't part of the gang until after the old lady died.

"Yes," said Grace. "She got the house from her uncle, who died years ago. I expect most of this stuff was his."

Ma and Nana came in then with their tape measures.

"What kind of curtains would you like, Grace?" asked Ma. "Have you decided on a color yet?"

"I like purple best," said Grace.

"You can't have purple on the walls, though, Grace," said Ma. "It'd drive you crazy within a week."

Kester and Vince and Maria were coming in with the toolbox; they had reached Grace's room on their round of removing window bars.

"I like purple myself," said Vince. "It would take a lot of purple to make me crazy."

"Can I make a suggestion?" asked Crishell. "If you had a light matching color on the walls, like lavender, you could have real purple in the curtains and that wouldn't be so hard to change if you got tired of it."

"Good idea," said Vince. "Now let's get those bars down."

"Why did she have so many bars and locks?"

asked Crishell, as the metal grill came away, letting the sun in.

"Gerda Myerson was afraid," said Nana, shaking her head. "She had a terrible time during the war in Germany. Her whole family was wiped out by the Nazis and she was the only one left. When her uncle died, she had the house barred up to make her feel safe."

"Do you think she'd mind about all the changes we're making?" asked Grace.

"No," said Ma. "I think she'd be pleased to have young people living here again. You know how she liked you children."

Grace looked around "her" room, which was now rather full of people: all five gang members, Ma, Nana and Vince. Even Paw-Paw seemed quite at home. She closed her eyes and tried to imagine it transformed with the bunk beds Ma had promised her, bright walls and new curtains.

───── ⌘ ─────

It took all term, but by the Easter holidays Mrs. Myerson's house was transformed. All the window bars were down and there was only the normal amount of locks and bolts to keep a house secure. Nana took a big chest of drawers from Mrs. Myerson's old bedroom, one of the triple mirrors and a fancy umbrella stand from the hall. All the other furniture was sold to an antique shop, and with the money Nana bought a new sofa for the old apartment and a new washing machine and fridge for the house.

Every room was now painted and all the old carpets cleaned. Grace's room had lavender walls and pine bunk beds, a chest of drawers and a small desk. There were purple and white striped curtains at the window and duvet covers made of the same material. In the corner, where the big wardrobe used to be, was a clothes bar with a canvas cover. There were bookshelves (put up by Vince) and a full-length mirror and a brightly colored rug on the clean, gray carpet.

Everything smelled fresh and new; the only things left from the old room were the castle prints on the wall, which were now in new white frames. Apart from the fact that it was very tidy, it looked like a young girl's room. Crishell had helped a lot.

"And there's plenty of space for you to have someone to stay," pointed out Ma, for the umpteenth time.

Grace knew that Ma and Vince had done more for her room than any other. They still hadn't gotten new curtains up anywhere but the living room, and she was the only one whose bookshelves had been put up. She knew how keen they were for her to like it, and she did.

"It's great," she said. "I can't wait to show it to Aimee. When can she come and stay?"

"Well," said Ma. "I've already had a word with Carol about that. How would you like Aimee to come and stay here with you and Nana while Vince and I are on our honeymoon?"

"Great!" said Grace, but it reminded her how close the wedding was. Only a week away!

In the meantime, moving day arrived. On the weekend, the whole gang came around to help, together with Maria's mom's boyfriend and two friends of Vince's from work. There was no moving truck because the two homes were so close together, but that made it even harder work. The four men carried all the furniture that was moving from the apartment to the house and the heaviest boxes.

Kester could carry heavy boxes too and all the children helped with the many, many bags and heaps of things. It was a cold, crisp day but soon everyone was sweating and pulling off their coats and woolly sweaters.

"Your room looks as if a hurricane has hit it," Maria said to Grace.

"It's because I can't decide what to take to the new house and what to leave behind," said Grace. "I was going to take all my books but the shelves here look so bare without them."

"Well, put some back," said Crishell.

"Shall I take all my Harry Potters and Jackie Wilsons?" asked Grace, sitting in the middle of a heap of books. "Suppose I come back here for the night and want to read one of them again?"

"Then you can bring it with you, can't you?" said Maria.

"Yes, and you'll be close enough to your house to go back and get anything you forget," said Crishell.

Both girls had rooms they used in their father's new homes, so they were much more experienced at this kind of thing than Grace. In the end, she put all her fairy tales and picture books back on the shelves and packed all the longer storybooks in cardboard boxes. But there were still all the clothes and soft toys and decorations. It took all day Saturday and even then, they weren't ready to sleep in the new house.

Grace went to bed in her old room that night, missing the things that had already been taken to the house. She hugged her old blue rabbit and then felt sad that she had decided not to take him with her. Or the pink teddy. Or the cuddling koalas velcroed together.

I wish everything could be less complicated, thought Grace, and went straight to sleep.

———— ∞ ————

"OK," said Vince next morning, rubbing his hands. "Today we are definitely going to move into the new house!"

"Except me," said Nana. "I'll be staying put."

"But won't you be dreadfully lonely, Nana?" said Grace.

"No, child. I'll be fine," said Nana. "I'll have

Paw-Paw for company and it will be quite nice to have some peace and quiet after all the kerfuffle of the last few weeks."

But Paw-Paw the cat was nowhere to be seen; he didn't think changes were at all exciting and he didn't understand what was going on.

It was another hard day's work, but at last everything was in the right place. Nana wasn't allowed to do any of the carrying, because she was an old lady and had broken her ankle the year before. So she cooked a big meal to thank all the helpers. Kester ate mounds of mashed potatoes and chicken and gravy.

At last everyone but the family was gone and it was time for Grace and Ma to move into their new home. Vincent wouldn't be joining them until after the wedding. Nana came to the gate with them and gave them all a big hug.

"Now, don't forget, I'll be over right after breakfast to look after you while Ma's at work," she told Grace. "Some things don't change!"

At that moment, Paw-Paw came through

the gate in the other direction; he had been hiding under the bushes in Mrs. Myerson's old garden.

"There you are, you naughty boy," said Nana. "I expect you want your dinner too." The cat wound around her legs, and she waved, and the two of them walked back to the apartment where the back door was open, casting a wedge of lemon-colored light into the back garden.

"Ready, Grace?" asked Ma.

Grace took a deep breath and nodded.

And then the two of them walked through the gate to their new home.

Grace Goes Up the Aisle

It felt very strange to Grace, waking up in her new room next morning. There was no Paw-Paw kneading her chest and purring, no Nana calling her to breakfast, and the room felt unfamiliar and stank of paint.

For a moment Grace felt like another person, and then she smelled bacon and mushrooms cooking. She grabbed her robe, ran down the stairs and found Vincent making breakfast on their new stove. He had come over early to drive Ma to work at the hospital.

"Morning, Grace," he said cheerfully. He was wearing one of Nana's flowery aprons.

Grace giggled. "You look funny," she said.

"Doesn't he?" said Ma, coming into the kitchen yawning. But she was smiling. "I think we'll have to find you something a bit more masculine to wear if you're going to take up cooking."

"Don't you think Lucie's apron suits me?"

asked Vince, pirouetting on the spot, then grabbing Ma round the waist and waltzing her round the kitchen.

Grace watched them dancing and laughing together and felt a bit more normal. Perhaps she was going to like the new person she was becoming. She went over to supervise the frying pan.

There was a knock at the back door and Nana's dear, familiar face looked around the kitchen door. Grace rushed up and gave her a big hug.

"Are you all right, Nana? Not too lonely?"

"I'm fine, honey," said Nana.

"Let me get you a plate," said Grace, seeing the table was set for three.

"No, that's OK," said Nana, sitting in the fourth chair. "I've had my breakfast already. But I'll take a cup of Vince's good coffee, if he's making it."

It felt so weird to have Nana sitting at their table like a visitor, instead of being the person making the meal, that Grace was glad when Vincent looked at his watch and said, "Hadn't you better be getting ready, Ava?" and

Ma said, "Heavens! Is that the time?" as she did every morning.

This is what our life is going to be like, thought Grace, once they're married. We'll be like a storybook family again with a mother and a father—like Pa's family in Africa.

After she and Nana had cleared away the breakfast, there was a ring at the doorbell. It was the first time Grace had answered the door for anyone in the new house and it reminded her of the first time they had called on Mrs. Myerson. Especially when she saw it was Raj and the others. They were thinking about that first time too.

"Do you remember when we were ghost busters?" asked Raj.

"And we thought this house was haunted?" said Maria.

"And Yowler yowled and we thought it was a ghost?" said Kester.

And now Yowler lives with Aimee and I live here, thought Grace. "Come through to the back," she said out loud.

They were out in the garden where Maria

had found the red flower when they played safaris and secret gardens at Mrs. Myerson's. Now there were daffodils everywhere and green buds on the bushes. And, most different of all, there was Vince's "magic gate" between this garden and Grace's old one.

Nana bustled back and forth through the gate with armfuls of cloth; she was still finishing off curtains on her sewing machine. The children helped her to hang them, Kester being specially useful because of his height.

"Thank you, dears," said Nana, when it was all done. "I needed to get that out of the way so I can finish the clothes for the wedding— I can't believe we have less than a week!"

"What's your Ma going to wear?" Crishell asked Grace.

"She bought a cream silk suit and a hat to match, with a cute little veil," said Grace. "And Nana's making me a purple dress with white butterflies on it."

"Yes, and I've got to finish my own dress, too," said Nana.

"Can we help?" asked Maria. She and

Crishell were interested in everything about the wedding, but Raj and Kester were quite bored by it all.

"It's a girl thing," said Raj. "I bet Vince doesn't spend all his time thinking about the wedding."

"Well, as a matter of fact," said Nana, "he's on a strict diet, to make sure he fits into his new suit. So maybe he thinks about it every time he says 'no' to a doughnut."

"But I bet he doesn't talk about it all the time," said Kester. "All the man has to do is show up, wear a new suit and remember the ring."

The three girls rolled their eyes in exasperation, but secretly Grace agreed with the boys a little bit. What with all the house moving and the preparations for the wedding, she had felt just a tad neglected this term; she couldn't even count on Nana's attention in the same way any more, since she was always so busy. And Paw-Paw felt the same as Grace. Even though he was supposed to be living in the apartment with Nana, he took to visiting Grace in the house—not bothering with the new gate, of course—where he could be sure of getting a cuddle.

"I know how you feel," she told him, burying her face in his purring, furry chest. "Weddings take up too much time. I can't remember the last time Nana told me one of her stories."

The day of the wedding dawned bright and sunny. Ma had refused to go to church in Nana's old car and didn't want to drive herself in her own, slightly newer one. So a specially hired white car with ribbons came and took them to the church. Nana sat in the front and Grace sat in the back with Ma, both of them keeping very still and stiff so as not to crush their new clothes.

Their church was only a few streets away and, when they got there, the bells were ringing.

"That's for you, Ava," said Nana.

"And for Vince," said Grace, wanting to be fair.

"Oh, Grace," said Ma, giving her a hug in spite of their clothes. "You do like him, don't you? You do think I'm doing the right thing?"

It's bit late to ask me that, thought Grace.

But out loud she said, "Of course I do," because actually she did like Vince now. He was funny and kind and he made Ma happy. It wouldn't be the same as having Papa live with them again but it would still be OK.

"No crying, now!" said Nana. "Think of all that time you spent making up your face." But Grace saw Ma brush away a small tear.

They got out of the car and Nana adjusted Ma's little hat-veil. Nana was going to "give her away," and Grace was the only bridesmaid, so the three of them went through the church door together and the organist launched into a wedding march. Grace wondered if he had a special mirror so that he could see when a bride arrived.

It did seem an awfully long way up the aisle to where Vince was already waiting. The church wasn't packed, because only close friends and a few of the usual Sunday congregation had been invited.

"It's my second time, remember," Ma had said. "We're so lucky that our vicar agreed to marry us in church at all."

Walking behind Ma and Nana, Grace could

see that they were both a bit trembly. She looked ahead and saw the big reassuring figure of Vince; he beamed at them and gave Grace the smallest of winks.

"Dearly beloved . . ." began the vicar.

Grace had never been to a wedding before and it felt funny that her first one should be her own ma's. She sat next to Nana, who was looking lovely in her new rose-print dress, and held her hand tightly all the way through.

It seemed no time at all before they were walking back down the aisle again, with Ma and Vince in front and Grace and Nana walking behind. The organ blazed out another march, the bells rang and in a moment they were outside the church and Vince was kissing Ma and Grace was fumbling in her little purple bag for her confetti. She and Nana threw it all over the newlyweds and it got in their hair and in Ma's hat and down Vince's collar.

The big white car was waiting for them and Grace didn't know what to do; she thought Ma and Vince would get in and drive off as a couple without her. But no such thing happened. In fact, Vince showed her in after Ma so that she sat between them while Nana rode in front again.

A few minutes after they got back to the house, their friends started arriving for the party, but it was long enough for Vince to carry Ma, laughing and protesting, across the threshold. And then he took Grace aside and gave her a little velvet box.

"What's this?" asked Grace, surprised. It looked just like the box Ma's engagement ring came in.

"Didn't you know that the bridegroom is supposed to give the bridesmaid a present?" said Vince, smiling at her.

Grace didn't know that and she opened the box. Inside was a pair of silver earrings with a dark, sparkly stone in the middle. Grace's eyes opened wide.

"For me?" she said. "They look so grown-up."

"They're amethysts," said Vince. "It was the only purple stone I could find. Do you like them?" He looked quite anxious.

"I love them," said Grace, and she took out the little silver hoops she was wearing and put

the new earrings in right away. Then she gave Vince a thank-you kiss and his smile grew even broader.

All the gang were invited, with their parents, and the gate between the two gardens was left open so that people could sit in both of them to eat and drink. The friends wandered around with glasses of fruit punch and plates of goodies. Kester's was piled high but Crishell didn't touch much of hers. Her mother was there too and Crishell never dared eat much when she was around.

"It was a lovely ceremony," said someone. "And doesn't Ava look beautiful?"

"Do you wish she had a long white dress?" Maria asked Grace.

"Not really," said Grace. "I mean, she did all that when she married my papa—I've seen the photos—and they still broke up."

"Same with mine," said Kester.

"And mine," agreed Crishell.

"Hey," said Raj. "I'm the only one whose parents still live together."

"And Aimee," said Maria.

"But she's not really one of us any more,

is she?" said Raj. Then, seeing the looks he was getting, "What? I only mean . . ."

"We know what you mean," said Kester, giving him a little thump.

"He's right," said Grace, "but I don't want to think about that today. Or about divorces. Now it's time to celebrate!"

While the party was still in full swing, Vince and Ma got in an ordinary cab to leave for the station. But Ma got out again for another hug with Grace.

"Come on, Ava—we'll miss our train," said Vince.

"Don't forget to throw your bouquet!" said Nana.

Ma hurled her posy of cream and pink roses out of the car window as it was driving away. It sailed high up in the air and everyone surged forward to catch it as it fell, except Grace, who was standing in the street waving at the back of the departing car.

"Owzat!" shouted Kester, as he made a perfect catch, then blushed as he realized everyone was laughing. Quickly he handed the flowers over to Nana, who said,

"That's nice, dear. I'll put them in some water."

Then she called out to Grace, "Come back, honey. There's still a whole lot of party going on."

Grace in Memory Lane

The morning after the wedding, Grace woke up to find Paw-Paw on her chest. He was very happy that all the guests had gone away and very pleased that Grace and Nana were sleeping in the same house again.

"It's just like old times, isn't it, Nana?" said Grace, as they had breakfast at the kitchen table together. "Like any other school holidays when Ma's at work and you look after me."

"Yes, honey," said Nana. "Just as long as you remember it's also a new time, and your Ma will be back in a week with her new husband."

But today, Aimee's parents were bringing her to stay for the rest of the week.

Grace and Aimee had known each other since nursery school. Their mothers had met in the hospital when they were having their babies. The past term had been so weird for Grace, not having Aimee around. On the first day back after the Christmas holidays, it had been great to be back in Ms. Woollacott's class with Maria and Raj and Kester and Crishell, but to Grace it still felt as if there was an Aimee-shaped hole in her life.

They talked on their cell phones every Sunday and Grace knew it was even harder for Aimee, settling into a new school in a new town and having to live in a new house. The first Sunday of the term, Aimee had said, "It's awful, Grace. I don't know anyone and I miss you and the gang so much."

That made Grace feel really guilty. At least she still had Maria and Kester and Raj and her new friend Crishell, but poor Aimee had to start all over again. She sounded more cheerful as the weeks went by and had even mentioned a girl called Ayesha a few times. And they always tried to get Paw-Paw and Yowler to say "hi" over the phone—though Yowler was much better at this game than Paw-Paw was.

Carol and Joe dropped Aimee off in the middle of Sunday morning and stayed just long enough for coffee and a guided tour of the new house.

"I can't believe it," said Carol. "It's so different from when Mrs. Myerson lived here—so light and airy with all the bars down."

At first Grace and Aimee felt a bit shy together.

"How's Yowler?" asked Grace.

"He's fine," said Aimee. "He's turning into the boss cat of the neighborhood. How's Paw-Paw?"

"He's fine too," said Grace. "Only he didn't like all the wedding fuss. He's supposed to live with Nana in our old apartment, but he's here with us this week. I think he's in the garden. He can't quite believe that Yowler's gone from the house."

"Everything's gone, isn't it?" said Aimee. "It's not Mrs. Myerson's any more."

"Everything's changed since Christmas," said Grace. "But it's only a few months since you lived just around the corner."

"I know," said Aimee.

Nana was cooking lunch for Grace and Aimee and all the gang and it wasn't long before they arrived. It was just like the old days except that, now they had Crishell as well, there were six of them instead of five.

Maria and the boys were very glad to see Aimee and were soon chatting about old times. But Crishell was withdrawn. They spent the morning in what they still thought of as Mrs. Myerson's garden. It was another really sunny day.

Nana brought them out some apple juice and chocolate cookies.

"No, thank you," said Crishell, almost as snootily as when she first came to school. "I'm not supposed to eat between meals."

"I like the gate," said Aimee, to cover up the awkwardness.

"It was Vince's invention," said Grace. "He says it's a magic gateway."

That gave her an idea. "Why don't we go through it now?" she said. She had the strangest feeling that if she went with her friends back through the gate, everything would be the same as last year. It would be like a real time machine.

And in a way she was right. Paw-Paw was stretched out in the sunshine in their old garden. Grace could almost believe that they were going to have their lunch in the apartment with Ma and Nana and that Vince was still just a friend at Ma's work.

Crishell suddenly whispered to Grace, "I'm going home. I don't want to be part of your trip down memory lane. I'll give my mom a ring."

Grace felt horrible, but just being back in the old garden with the five of them was so good that she was able to push Crishell to the back of her mind. They played time travelers until lunchtime, reliving all their old adventures. Then they all gathered around the table in Mrs. Myerson's old dining room. It looked very different now, with the bars off its windows and light floaty curtains instead. Nana had put out one of her cheerful, flowery tablecloths and a big vase of tulips stood in the middle of the table.

"It's a shame Crishell wasn't feeling well," she said. "That child doesn't get enough home-cooked food, if you ask me."

But then she took the lids off the dishes and the lunch smelled so good that everyone forgot about Crishell.

After all the washing up had been done,

the gang played ball in the garden while Nana had a nap. And that night, when the two girls went to bed in Grace's new bunks, they felt almost back to normal, even though it was a different bedroom. Aimee was very impressed by all the space and Grace's new color scheme. They stayed awake half the night talking.

"I've forgotten what it's like to have a mom and a dad," Grace whispered to Aimee. "And ever since Christmas there's been nothing but jobs and busy-ness and arrangements."

"But it'll be different now that you've finished moving and the wedding's over, won't it?" said Aimee comfortingly in the dark, and Grace thought again about how much she had missed her.

For the rest of the week Grace felt more settled than she had for some time. The gang was reunited, her best friend was with her again and she had shared her secret worries.

The only fly in the ointment was Crishell. Grace telephoned her a couple of times but she didn't want to spend time with the gang while Aimee was still there, and sounded a bit annoyed.

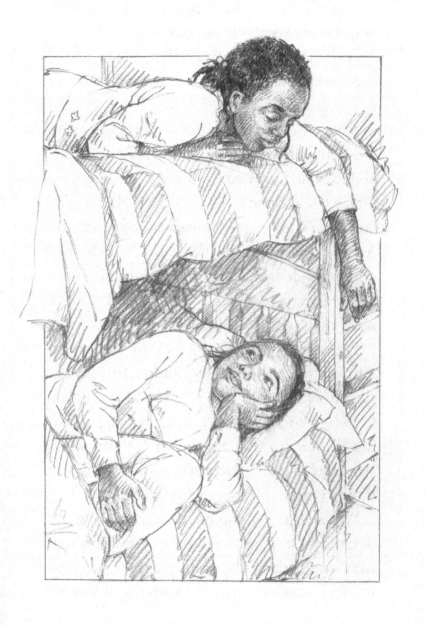

"I don't want to be a third wheel," she said. "I'll see you when we go back to school."

And the funny thing was that, by the end of the week, Grace was missing Crishell almost as much as she had missed Aimee before. It was lovely to be back with her oldest friend who knew her so well, but Aimee knew nothing about what they had been doing all term and Grace felt she had to entertain her all the time and didn't like to leave her on her own and read a book. When she was with Crishell, they often sat side by side reading their books and it was perfectly companionable, but it didn't seem right with a visitor.

Grace felt torn in half, the way she had in Africa, when she was beginning to like her stepmother, Jatou, and her ma had rung up from home to talk to her. There was no avoiding the reality that by the end of the week, Aimee would be gone again and Grace would have to make things up with Crishell.

When Aimee's parents turned up the next Saturday, Grace was almost relieved. Though they would always be friends, Aimee was now in some ways less easy to be with than Crishell.

"Call me tomorrow," said Aimee, waving out the window of the car.

"I will," Grace called back, and then she went back into the house and spent the rest of the morning curled up with a book.

But in an hour or two, there was the sound of a key in the lock and Vince and Ma were back.

"Another present for me?" asked Grace, when the hugs and hellos were over and Ma gave her a little parcel.

There was a silver charm bracelet for Grace with a palm tree charm to start her off and a cream straw hat with roses and a pink ribbon for Nana.

"That's lovely," said Nana. "I can wear it to church with the dress I made for the wedding."

"That's what we thought," said Vince, looking pleased with himself.

Even Paw-Paw got a new red collar.

Over lunch, Grace kept looking at Ma's and Vince's shiny new gold wedding rings. I wonder where Ma has put Papa's old ring? she thought.

And then, after lunch, Nana eased herself

up out of her chair and said, "Well I'd better be getting back to the apartment. Shall I strip my bed in the spare room, Ava?"

"No, leave it," said Ma. "You might want to sleep over again soon."

"Yes, please do, Nana," said Grace.

"I'm sure I shall, child," said Nana, "but I think I should spend a while setting the apartment to rights. And I want Paw-Paw to settle down. That cat doesn't know whether he's coming or going."

"Then can I come and see you, Nana?" asked Grace.

"Any time, honey," said Nana. "You don't have to wait to be asked. It's your other home."

But when she watched Nana walking through the gate, it didn't seem like a magic time machine to Grace any more. There had been some big changes in her life. But she was determined not to be sad about them. "I think I must be growing up," she said to herself, and she was surprised at the thought.

Grace and the
Gingerbread House

It took a few days for Grace and Crishell to get back to normal after Aimee's visit, when they all went back to school after the Easter holidays. The atmosphere was decidedly frosty on Crishell's side. But the gang still sat together for lunch and the others were still bringing extra food to school in case Crishell needed more than she had in her lunchbox.

It was Thursday before she accepted anything and then it was from Maria, not Grace.

"Would you like a sandwich, Crishell?" asked Maria. "My mom put in two today and I'm stuffed."

"Thanks," said Crishell and, though she ate only half of it, the others could all see that she was still really hungry after her meal of carrot and celery and low-fat hummus and yogurt and grapes.

They had all noticed how much thinner

Crishell looked after the Easter holiday. If she had been allowed, Crishell would have eaten as much as any of the gang, except perhaps Kester, but her mother had a real bee in her bonnet about weight gain and obviously had been keeping a careful eye on Crishell's diet while she was at home. Grace felt guilty, because if Crishell had spent more time with them, they would have been able to feed her up and it was Grace's fault that she had stayed away.

"Do you want half my chocolate?" offered Kester.

Crishell smiled for the first time that week. She knew how hard it was for Kester to give away food. But she shook her head.

"Take it for later," he said heroically, and Crishell put the remains of the bar in her book bag.

"We're going to have a treat this afternoon," said Ms. Woollacott. "Do you remember La Tasha's uncle made a video of our Christmas play? Tasha has brought the tape in today. So after lunch, if you all work hard this morning, we can watch it."

They couldn't wait to see *Waking Beauty*, which is what Grace and Crishell called their version of the fairy tale. It was very up-to-date, with the fairies at the christening giving gifts like friendship and soccer skills, and Grace was a very wicked fairy called Malicia Badheart.

When they watched the video, it was strange to see themselves all dressed up in their costumes.

"Oh, no, I look awful!" said Natalie, putting her hands over her face, but she really wanted her friends Daisy and Lynnette to say how pretty she had been as Slumberella.

"You look lovely," they said straight away, and Russell said, "Yeah!" rather too loudly, so that all the boys laughed and kept teasing him.

Grace secretly thought that Natalie had been a bit boring as the Sleeping Beauty, but then she didn't think it was much of a part. She much preferred the Wicked Fairy. But it was strange to think what her life had been like at the time of the play. Ma and Vince hadn't been engaged then and she and Grace and Nana were all still living in the

49

apartment. It made Grace feel as if she had slept a hundred years, like Slumberella, and woken up to find everything different.

"What do you think, Grace?" Ms. Woollacott was asking, and Grace realized that she hadn't been listening to the class discussion at all.

"Stop daydreaming, you lot," said Ms. Woollacott. "We were talking about putting on another play. I'd have thought that would be just your sort of thing."

Grace was immediately all ears.

"You were all so good at Christmas," Ms. Woollacott explained, "that we were wondering about getting this class to put on some more plays based on fairy tales, so that the little kids could get to know the stories."

Grace's gang thought this was a wonderful idea.

"I want you all to write down the titles of as many fairy stories as you can think of when you get home," said Ms. Woollacott. "Then we can discuss them tomorrow and decide how many we can turn into plays."

This new idea cheered Grace up a lot. Now at last there was something to think about that had nothing to do with moving or weddings or losing her best friend.

"Can Maria and Crishell come for a sleepover on Saturday?" she asked Ma that night.

"Of course," said Ma. "There's plenty of room."

By the time that Maria and Crishell came on Saturday, their class had decided on *Hansel and Gretel*, *Red Riding Hood* and *Beauty and the Beast* for the three fairy tales they wanted to perform. They were going to keep them short—Grace and Crishell would write them—and put them on in assemblies for the little ones in the last week of the term. All their own literacy class work would be connected to this project.

The three girls went to bed early, but not to sleep. As well as the usual preparations for a midnight feast, there was the strangeness of staying in a new room. Maria had often slept over at Grace's apartment with Aimee and it had always been a bit of a squash in her room, involving sleeping bags and nowhere to put your feet. But now there was plenty of space for everyone; there was even a little trundle bed that rolled out from under the bunks. It had its own purple-and-white striped duvet and Grace was going to sleep there, while her friends had the bunks. But for now, they were all sitting on the top one.

"I bet Natalie wants to be Gretel *and* Red Hiding Hood *and* Beauty too," said Maria.

"Let her," said Grace. "I'd much rather be the witch and the wolf and the Beast."

"You can't be all those," said Maria, laughing.

"And you've just been the Wicked Fairy," pointed out Crishell, "which is more or less the same as the witch. We'll have to share the good parts."

"Like chocolate," said Grace. "Let's see what you've brought."

The girls emptied their bags on the top bunk. Crishell hadn't brought very much, because her mother wouldn't let her eat junk food and was still watching her like an eagle at home. But Maria had brought quite a bit and

Nana had made brownies for them, so there was plenty to share.

"Mmmn," said Maria. "I'd rather have chocolate than a good part. I don't really like acting. Perhaps I could do the costumes or something?"

Crishell didn't say anything. She couldn't understand anyone not wanting to act. But Grace was used to Maria and knew that she didn't like people looking at her; Maria was the one who had been an urchin with the boys when the gang had all been in *Annie*, because she didn't want any words to learn.

"That's OK, Maria," she said. "There'll be all sorts of stuff to do besides acting, like makeup, for instance."

Maria brightened. "We could start practicing now," she said. "I brought some."

"So did I," said Crishell.

By the time Ma came to tell them to turn the light out, there were three very alarming-looking girls, with lots of eyeliner and red lips, giggling into hand mirrors.

Ma smiled at them. "That takes me back," she said. "I used to have makeover-sleepovers with my friends when I was your age too. But just like you, I had to wash all the makeup off before going to bed."

"They're not ordinary makeovers, Ma," said Grace. "We're practicing being witches."

"Well make sure you're in bed by midnight, because that's the witching hour!" said Ma. "And I might turn you all into pumpkins if you disturb my sleep."

The first play to be written was *Hansel and Gretel*. Grace didn't have a part: Russell was Hansel and Natalie was Gretel. La Tasha was the wicked witch with the gingerbread house and was enjoying herself enormously.

Grace wrote the script with Crishell and made sure they all said the right words. Kester and Maria made a great oven out of orange crates for La Tasha to crawl into, to show Natalie what to do. And they all painted a paper backdrop of the cottage made of goodies, with a door that really opened.

"Looks good enough to eat, doesn't it?" said

Russell to La Tasha, as he finished painting a ring-doughnut door knocker.

But La Tasha, who was used to Russell and didn't mind being teased about her size, just said, "Yeah, bring it on—I'm starving!"

"It's Crishell that looks as if she's starving," said Russell nastily, just loud enough for her to hear.

The gang pricked their ears up. They had had trouble with Russell bullying their friends before. He never used physical violence; words were his weapon and these had found their target. Crishell looked really upset.

"Cut it out, Russell," said Kester.

Russell left off for a while, but the next time they had rehearsal, they were doing the scene where Hansel is in a cage being fattened up and holds out a bone for the witch to feel. Russell was inside an enclosure made of classroom chairs, holding out a rubber dog bone while La Tasha cackled, "Surely he must be fatter than that. I've been feeding him pork and beans for weeks—not too mention all the chocolate pudding and custard!"

"No," said Natalie. "You can't eat poor Hansel yet—he's thin as a rake."

When the scene was over, Russell said loudly to Natalie, "It should be Crishell playing Hansel—she's thin as a rake."

And Natalie giggled, because she liked Russell. They both looked at Crishell and she hid her face in her hands.

"That's it," said Grace. "I've had enough of Russell. I thought we had set him straight last term with that *Diamonds and Toads* story, but he's as bad as ever. I'm going to Ms. Woollacott."

Crishell begged her not to, but once Grace had made her mind up to do something, it almost always happened. She stayed back after class and asked to speak to their teacher.

"What is it, Grace?" asked Ms. Woollacott. "Is it about the play? I think it's going really well."

"No," said Grace, very quickly, so that there would be no turning back. "It's about bullying."

Five Heads Are Better than One

Ms. Woollacott's pleased expression changed immediately. "Oh, Grace, I'm sorry. Do you want to tell me about it?"

"I'll have to go and get my nana first," said Grace. "She'll be waiting for me in the playground."

"Well, you do that and I'll wait for you here," said Ms. Woollacott.

By the time Grace had told Nana what it was about, she was feeling far less brave. Her heart was pounding and Nana was looking very worried. But Ms. Woollacott put them at their ease.

"I'm sorry to hear that you've been bullied, Grace," she said. "You know, we have a very strict school policy about bullying," she said to Nana.

"It's not me," Grace told her teacher. "He hasn't done anything to me—at least, not for ages. But he's horrible to most girls and now he's started picking on Crishell."

"Who exactly are we talking about?" asked Ms. Woollacott.

"Russell Hunter," said Grace. "He doesn't often hurt people by hitting them but he does it with words."

Ms. Woollacott looked thoughtful.

"Was that what your *Diamonds and Toads* story was about last Christmas?" she asked.

"Yes," said Grace. "I don't think he's ever forgiven me and Crishell for showing him up in class. But he doesn't dare say anything to me anymore because he knows I'd tell."

"Which is what you are doing, Grace," said Ms. Woollacott. "That's the right thing to do. But we have a problem. We can't take any action unless the person being bullied, or their parent, makes the complaint."

"You mean you can't do anything about Russell?" said Grace. Her heart sank, because she didn't think that Crishell would ever admit what was going on to the teachers.

"I shall certainly mention it to the Principal," said Ms. Woollacott. "And I suggest you have a talk with Crishell. If she comes to me, we can ask Russell's parents to come in and tell them what's been happening, so that we can decide what to do about it."

"OK," said Grace. "I'll try."

"And I promise I'll keep my eyes open in class," said Ms. Woollacott. And my ears."

On the way home, Grace was very quiet.

"You did a good thing, Grace," said Nana. "Don't give up because it hasn't worked yet."

"It didn't do any good, though," objected Grace. "Crishell will never talk to anyone at school about it. She'd have to tell them what Russell said and then her mother would be in trouble."

"Well, maybe it's time that someone knew what's happening in Crishell's home, Grace," said Nana seriously. "It's not natural for a mother to stop her child from eating."

"It's all because Crishell's dad ran away with a slim young model," said Grace. "Now her mother thinks you've got to be thin to be beautiful."

Nana snorted. "That leaves me out then! And most of my friends. And I think they're all beautiful."

"You're beautiful too," said Grace, smiling. "You wouldn't be my nana if you were all skinny like a model."

"I couldn't do it, honey," said Nana. "I like my food too much."

"Me too!" said Grace. "What's for dinner?"

———⚬⚬⚬———

Ms. Woollacott was as good as her word. The very next day in assembly, the Principal, Mrs. Cavanagh, talked about bullying. "It's not just hitting and hurting people that is bullying," she said. "There's an old expression: 'Sticks and stones may break my bones but words will never hurt me.' Now, I want you to know that I think that expression is wrong. Words can hurt as much as sticks and stones and this kind of bullying is just as serious as the physical kind."

Everyone in Grace's class swiveled their eyes toward Russell and she was pleased to see that Ms. Woollacott had noticed. But she was less pleased to see that Russell was smirking, as if he thought it was cool to be cruel and even cooler for everyone to know it.

"I'd like to knock that stupid smile off his face," fumed Kester, on their way back to class.

"But then you would be as bad as he is," said Maria.

"No way," said Raj. "Fighting isn't the same as bullying. Because it's fair if you're both the same size and age, and bullying isn't fair."

"Russell isn't the same size as Kester, though, is he?" said Crishell. "No one is."

Kester didn't mind. "Then Raj or Grace could beat him up," he said. "They're the same size and just as strong."

"No one is going to beat anyone up," said Grace patiently. "But we are going to get Russell somehow. Crishell, you have to tell Ms. Woollacott what's going on."

But Crishell just shook her head and looked miserable.

That day in rehearsal, Russell behaved himself; he couldn't really do anything else because Ms. Woollacott was keeping a close watch on him. But he spent a lot of time whispering to Natalie and she did a lot of giggling and looking at Crishell.

La Tasha was fed up with them. "Why

doesn't your gang do something about that creep?" she said to Grace at lunchtime.

And that gave Grace an idea. She said to Crishell, "The next time it happens with Russell, would you go to Ms Woollacott if we all came with you?"

Crishell looked startled. "Maybe," she said. "But maybe he'll stop now that he knows the teachers are watching him."

Grace didn't say anything, but she didn't think Russell would give up his cruel ways.

The next week, they started rehearsals for *Red Riding Hood*. Lynnette, Natalie's best friend, was the little girl in the story and a girl called Sally was the grandmother. Kester was the wolf and he loved it, leaping and growling through the woods and then spotting Natalie with her basket of goodies. His favorite part was where he had pretended to eat Sally and was sitting up in the grandmother's bed wearing a frilly nightgown while Lynnette said, "What big teeth you have, Grandma!"

Robert was the woodcutter and he had an ax made of cardboard and tin foil. It was a bit flimsy so he had to remember not to hit Kester too hard. Sally was going to be hiding under the big frilly nightgown and would jump out when the woodcutter killed the wolf in the last scene.

Rehearsing that bit was a lot of fun and Grace was enjoying watching with La Tasha. Crishell was watching from the other side of the class. The nightgown belonged to La Tasha's mom, who was big like her. It had to be big to fit Kester, and Sally had to hide inside it too.

"Good job we've got some fatsos in the class," someone whispered behind Crishell. "Imagine trying to fit two people into your nightdress."

Crishell kept looking at the action on the stage, determined not to respond.

"Stick insect," he hissed. "Anorexic! You'll never get a boyfriend. Who'd want to cuddle a bag of bones like you?"

Crishell burst into tears. On the other side of the room, Grace saw her and saw Russell sliding away with a pleased expression on his face. He always stopped when his victims began to cry.

"That's it," said Grace. "He's gone too far this time!"

"I wonder what he said," said La Tasha. "But she shouldn't let him upset her. It only makes him worse."

The rehearsal finished as Grace got to Crishell. Her friend was still shaking. "What did Russell say this time?" Grace demanded.

"Just more of the same," said Crishell. "Only a bit worse."

"It's not going to get any better unless we do something about him," said Grace. "We have to go to Ms. Woollacott."

Crishell hesitated. "Are you sure you'd all come with me?" she said.

Ms. Woollacott was surprised when she opened the staff room door to all five of them. But she realized immediately what it was about when she saw Crishell's tear-stained face. Grace, Maria, Kester and Raj were ranged on either side of her like bodyguards.

"Crishell wants to tell you something," said Grace.

<hr>

The next morning, Russell and his parents were in Mrs. Cavanagh's office with Crishell and her mother. The whole gang was outside. They weren't allowed to sit in on the meeting but there was no way they were going to wait in class while Crishell was in there. Ms. Woollacott had told them they could wait for her.

"I hope he gets expelled," said Kester.

"What good would that do?" said Grace.

"Yeah," said Maria. "He'd only end up in some other school where he could bully someone else."

"But they've got to do something," said Raj. "Otherwise he'll just keep doing it."

———— ✦ ————

Inside the office, Russell was having a very uncomfortable time. His father was furious at being called into school because of his son's bad behavior. Crishell's mother wasn't happy either. Crishell had told her everything that Russell had said and had cried so much that her mother was starting to think hard about what had been going on in their home.

Russell was no longer smiling; he looked really anxious. Crishell realized suddenly that he was afraid of his father.

"Leave him to me," the big man kept saying. "I'll deal with him at home."

"That's not the answer, Mr. Hunter," said Mrs. Cavanagh calmly. "First, since Russell has admitted that he has been bullying Crishell, he must write her a letter apologizing to her and promising not to do it again. But she is not the only student he has bullied. Russell seems to have quite a reputation for verbal cruelty."

"Huh!" snorted Russell's father. "Verbal cruelty! What sort of wimps are they if they can't take a bit of teasing? It's not as if he was bashing little kids."

"Mr. Hunter," said Mrs. Cavanagh, quite sharply. "We take all types of bullying equally seriously in this school. Russell will now be reported to the School Board and an eye will also be kept on him in this school and in his next. In addition, we want him to receive counseling. Do you agree to that?"

Russell's father muttered a bit, but his mother nodded. "He'll do it," she said. She looked a bit scared herself, thought Crishell.

Eventually the Hunters took Russell out of the office and Crishell's mother got up to leave too, but Mrs. Cavanagh stopped her.

"Sit down, if you would, Ms. Connor," she said. "I have been concerned about Crishell for some time. What Russell did was inexcusable, but your daughter really is very thin. Is there a problem you would like to talk about?"

To Crishell's horror, her mother burst into tears. Mrs. Cavanagh came around her desk and offered her a box of tissues.

"Would you like to go back to class, Crishell?" she asked. Crishell looked at her mother, who nodded and waved her away. "You go, darling. I'll be OK," she said.

And Crishell turned and fled from the room. She cannoned straight into the gang, who had seen Russell leaving with his head hanging.

"What happened?" said Grace.

"Oh, he owned up," said Crishell, "and he has to say sorry and go to counseling."

"So why are you crying?" asked Raj.

"It's probably relief," said Maria.

"And shock," added Kester. "Here, have my chocolate bar."

And Crishell accepted it and took a big bite.

Grace and the Bombshell

Grace and Crishell were eager to get on with writing their version of *Beauty and the Beast*.

"Her sisters were horrid to her, weren't they?" said Crishell.

"Yes," said Grace. "Mean and jealous. And they were greedy and selfish too, not doing chores when their father's fortune got lost."

"Makes you glad to be an only child, doesn't it?" said Crishell.

Grace thought about that.

"I'm not really an only child," she said. "Because I've got Neneh and Bakary, but they're so far away. I know they're only halves but they would feel like a real brother and sister if they lived nearer."

"But would you like to have brothers and sisters?" asked Crishell.

"Maybe. It could be fun sometimes. You and Maria are like sisters, though," said Grace. "And Aimee," she added loyally.

"That's different," said Crishell. "You can choose your friends but your brothers and sisters are just sort of dumped on you. You have to love them, or at least get along with them."

Julio was going to be the Beast and Maria was having a wonderful time working out his makeup and making him a cardboard mask. Beauty was a girl called Sophie and Raj was her father. Grace and Crishell volunteered to be the mean sisters and were really enjoying themselves.

Russell had been very quiet while the class was rehearsing *Beauty and the Beast*. Word had got around about what had happened and how he'd had to write Crishell a letter, but she hadn't shown it to anyone, not even Grace. He watched very carefully while Crishell and Grace were being the mean sisters. Crishell said, "Who does she think she is? Asking for a measly rose!"

"Yes," said Grace. "Beauty's trying to show us up, asking for something cheap when we wanted silks and satins."

"She's always sucking up to Daddy," said

Crishell, and Beauty pretended to cry because they had been horrible to her.

After rehearsal, Russell came up to the two girls a bit hesitantly.

"You don't need to rub it in," he said. "I've said I'm sorry. And I'm paying for it—as if you care."

"It's not about you, Russell," said Grace. "It's just the way the story is."

"Everything all right?" asked Ms. Woollacott, coming up to them.

"Fine," said Crishell.

"She's watching me all the time," said Russell, when Ms. Wollacott had gone away again.

"You can't be surprised," said Grace. "It serves you right."

But Crishell said, "Don't be too hard on him." She remembered what Russell's father had been like. He flashed her a grateful look.

"What's that all about?" asked Grace, but Crishell just shrugged.

That evening, Ma noticed Grace was a bit quiet.

"What's up?" she asked.

"Nothing," said Grace and tried to take an interest in the TV program Ma was watching.

She was not used to confiding in Ma; in the past Nana had always been there to talk to in the evenings. Now Nana went back to the apartment as soon as Ma and Vince got in from work. It was Vince who cooked their dinners now and, though they were much better than Ma's, they weren't quite as nice as Nana's.

It was another few days before Grace told Nana what was on her mind, as they drank lemonade outside. The gate was open and Paw-Paw played a game of wandering in and out between the two gardens.

"Do you think he thinks it's a time machine too?" asked Nana.

"If it was," said Grace, "then I'd go back with him to when things were simple."

"Aren't they simple now, then?"

"Well, in the old days it was our gang against people like Russell and Natalie. And now Crishell—who wasn't even in our gang this time last year—expects me to be nice to Russell. And that's after all the horrible things he said about her!"

Nana didn't answer right away. "You don't think she's right, do you?" said Grace.

"Your friend may have a point," said Nana. "There's no excuse for bullying, but that boy's bad behavior has brought something else to light that needed dealing with. Crishell's mother had a real eating problem and she was taking it out on the child. Now she can see she was wrong. Besides, if Crishell can forgive Russell, maybe you should give it a try too."

Grace didn't like this at all. She wanted Nana on her side.

"But it's not just her," she said. "He was horrible to Maria last winter and he makes little kids cry and he hurt me once when we were in third grade. And it was his idea that we should all go running off last winter when Crishell fell through the ice and nearly died."

"I'm not denying the boy has done bad things," said Nana. "Only wondering why, and wondering whether he should be given a second chance now that he's been found out and punished."

Grace said nothing. She knew that Crishell and her mother were seeing a counselor about eating disorders and that it had happened because of Russell's bullying. It was a very unusual case because Crishell herself wasn't anorexic; it was her mother who was hung up about her own figure and she was making Crishell diet too. Crishell didn't talk about it much, but Grace wondered if her friend might be secretly grateful to Russell for drawing attention to her problem. Then she remembered that Crishell had rather liked Russell before she joined Grace's gang. And of course Natalie was always hanging round him; he was a nice-looking boy.

"I think she has a crush on him," said Grace.

Nana looked astonished. "What kind of talk is that for a girl your age?" she said. "You're much too young to be thinking of boys that way."

"Honestly, Nana," said Grace, quite crossly. "Things are different now. Lots of the girls in my class are going out with boys."

"Going out?" said Nana, fanning herself with her magazine. "You mean—on dates?"

"Not really," said Grace, smiling in spite of herself. She just couldn't imagine Julio and Sophie on a date. "But they call it going out.

It means that they're girlfriend and boyfriend."

"Have you got a boyfriend, Grace?" asked Nana, and she looked so alarmed that Grace had to laugh.

"No, Nana," she said. "I'm not into that. But I do think Crishell might like Russell in that way. He's quite good-looking with his big gray eyes and floppy brown hair."

"Handsome is as handsome does," said Nana. It was one of her favorite expressions.

"Well, Russell doesn't *do* handsome," said Grace, "Even if he is it." And that was the end of their conversation.

Over the next few weeks, Grace saw that Crishell was putting on weight and looking healthier and happier. And she continued to be nice to Russell, going out of her way to show him that she didn't bear a grudge about his bullying.

"I don't know how she can stand him," Grace said to Maria, watching Crishell and Russell chatting over their math problem.

"Perhaps she likes him?" suggested Maria.

"You've noticed too?" said Grace.

They'd all been in the same class since

kindergarten, with very few changes. Aimee left and Crishell came and there were one or two other comings and goings but, by and large, this group of children shared a long history together and knew each other very well.

Now all the friendships and alliances seemed to be shifting. Lynnette and Natalie weren't speaking anymore and Grace thought they had probably argued over Russell. But it didn't seem to make any difference to him; he still preferred to spend time with Crishell. And that put a bit of a strain on Grace's gang.

Kester couldn't stand Russell. Being both big and gentle himself, he was very down on anyone who bullied weaker people and it didn't make any difference if it was only with words. And Raj thought whatever Kester thought; they had been best friends for years, just like Grace and Aimee.

The more Grace thought about it, the more she noticed something strange. It was true that some of the boys and girls were pairing off, but it also seemed to be be harder for boys and girls to be good friends.

In Grace's gang it all began with the

wedding. Kester and Raj were so fed up with all the talk about clothes and flowers and things that they stopped coming around to Grace's so often. And the girls were so caught up in it all that they had scarcely noticed.

But now that she was aware of all the other changes, Grace was noticing that the gang spent less time together at school. They all still sat together at lunchtime but often Kester and Raj went off to play soccer with Julio and Jason, and now they didn't usually ask the girls to join them.

Grace and Maria were quite good at soccer, though Crishell had never played with them much. But during all the wedding conversations they'd gotten out of the habit of playing with the boys. Grace realized that she was more often in a group of girls now, with Crishell and Maria and often La Tasha and Sophie as well, while Kester and Raj spent time with other boys. The gang still came around to Grace's on the weekend, but now she wondered how long that would last.

When Ma came to tuck her in one night, she said, " Grace, we need to have a little talk.

There's something I need to say to you."

Grace thought it might be about her moodiness of the last few weeks.

"I'm sorry I've been a bit grumpy," she said. "I'm just feeling a little unsettled."

"Oh, Grace," said Ma, with such a big sigh that Grace wondered if she was going to cry.

Grace put her arms round Ma. "What's the matter?" she asked.

"I'm sorry, Grace," said Ma. "I hope what I have to tell you isn't going to unsettle you even more."

Grace felt quite scared. "What's wrong? Nobody's ill, are they? Are you all right? And Vince? And Nana?"

She was completely unprepared for what came next.

"Everyone's fine," Ma said. "In fact, more than fine. Vince and I are going to have a baby."

Grace and the Right Story

Grace had no idea how she got through the next few weeks until the end of the term. She felt as if she were on autopilot. At school, she worked with Crishell and the others on their three fairy tales but she felt like a zombie, saying the words automatically.

All the gang noticed she was quiet but no one said anything. After all, Grace had been thoughtful for weeks now. But no one guessed that she had just been told about the biggest change of all. And she didn't feel ready to tell any of them, not even Maria.

At home, Vince and Ma seemed in a bit of a daze too. Grace spent most of her free time back at the old apartment with Nana. Nana was the only person she could talk to about the fact that she was going to get a brother or sister.

"Only it won't be, will it?" she said. "It will be a half one, like Neneh and Bakary in The Gambia."

"Not quite the same, honey," said Nana. "Because this new baby will live with you and Ma and Vince. It'll be like Neneh and Bakary in one way, but I'm guessing you'll feel much closer to it even than you do to your African family. You'll see him or her every day."

"But it'll be a baby and I'll be so much bigger—do you think it will even know I'm its sister?"

"Of course it will," said Nana. "Not right away, of course. But how lucky it's going to be to have a big sister like you!"

When Grace went back to the house that night, she decided to call Aimee on her cell phone. Aimee sounded surprised to hear from her when it wasn't a Sunday morning.

"Is there something wrong?" she asked straight away.

"Everything!" said Grace dramatically. "All the boys are going out with the girls. But the girls and boys don't spend any time together anymore."

Aimee could make little sense of this. But then Grace said, "And my Ma's going to have a baby!" and Aimee's big gasp at the other end was just what her friend needed to hear. Only then, Aimee spoiled it a bit by saying, "So soon?" as if it was only what Grace might have expected sooner or later.

"You mean, you guessed all along they'd have a baby?" asked Grace.

"Well, it is what happens, isn't it?" said Aimee. "People get married and then they have babies. At least they do if they're your ma and Vince's sort of age."

Grace knew that Aimee was right, but she also knew that she hadn't dreamt of it when Ma got engaged last Christmas and that was what was making her so mixed up. Grace hated things to happen that she hadn't already thought about.

She waited until Ma came to say goodnight and pretended to be already asleep. Then, when Ma's footsteps had gone downstairs and she heard the theme song of the late-night TV show Ma liked to watch with Vince, Grace tiptoed into their bedroom and picked up the extension phone. She dialed Papa's number in The Gambia, something she wouldn't have dared to do on her cell.

Jatou answered, and knew from the sound of Grace's voice that she wasn't just calling for a chat. "I'll get Antony," she said.

Grace knew it wasn't right to tell Papa before he had heard the news from Ma. But in the end she just had to get it off her chest.

There was a long silence at the other end.

"I expect Ava would have told me herself in the end," Papa said at last. "She took a long time to write to me about her engagement. But the main thing is, Grace, how do you feel about it?"

This was exactly what Grace wanted to hear, someone who understood that the most important thing about this new baby was how *she* felt about it. She talked to Papa for a long time, until she heard the TV theme again and realized she had been on the phone long distance for nearly an hour.

Whatever Papa said about how she would always be his and her ma's first child and how that made her special, it didn't alter the fact that he had done the same thing as Ma had—married someone else and then had a baby—two babies, in fact.

Perhaps Ma and Vince won't stop at one? thought Grace, as she hurried back to her own room. And the more she thought about it, the more certain she was that they wouldn't. She was sure Ma wouldn't have had only one child if Papa hadn't left. Now Grace saw the future mapped out ahead of her with more and more surprises in the shape of half brothers and half sisters. Their house would be as full as Maria's and she'd have to escape round to Crishell's all the time. Thank goodness Crishell really was an only!

Grace fell asleep dreaming of the Old Woman Who Lived in a Shoe, with screaming, tumbling, sticky brats leaning out of eyelet windows and rappelling down the shoelaces.

Next day at lunchtime she told the gang her news. They were wonderful. No one said, "How lovely!" or "Congratulations!" They were just the way they always had been.

Maria said, "Bad luck!" and gave her a hug. Raj said, "Oh no—your house will smell of diapers and we'll have to creep around being quiet when it's asleep."

Kester said, "You'll get used to it. It's just the shock, I expect."

And Crishell said, "You'll be a wicked stepsister!" which was quite the most cheerful thing Grace could think of, even though she did correct Crishell to "wicked halfsister."

In class they were still doing the fairy tale project, so Grace and Crishell worked together making a list of all the stories they knew involving halfsiblings and steps. There was *Diamonds and Toads*, which the girls had successfully retold in the winter term, turning the disagreeable stepsister into a boy, to get at Russell. Then *Cinderella*, of course, with the hateful ugly sisters, and their teacher had told them that in some versions of *Beauty and the Beast*, Beauty was a halfsister to the others.

Grace sat back astonished. "You see!" she told Crishell. "I'm doomed! The half or step *always* hates the new baby."

"It's only because you're used to being on your own in the family," said Crishell. "Like me. And Little Red Riding Hood and Snow White."

"Hang on," said Grace. "Isn't there one

about Snow White and Rose Red? Maybe they were halves or steps who got on well."

"Why don't we go to the library tomorrow and see what we can find?" suggested Crishell.

So they did. And as well as looking at all the fairy storybooks, they went on the Internet and looked up "Fairy tales+sisters" on the search engine.

They found *Snow White and Rose Red*, *Brave Molly Whuppie* and *Kate Crackernuts*, which were all stories about brave girls rescuing their sisters.

"It looks as if it will be all right if it's a girl," said Crishell. "Though Snow White and Rose Red were real sisters and so were Mollie and hers."

"What if it's a boy?" asked Grace.

"Well," said Crishell. "There's the lovely one about the girl whose brothers were turned into swans—not to mention *Hansel and Gretel*."

"I like the stories where the girls make things happen," said Grace. "Like Gretel tricking the witch and Beauty not being afraid of the Beast."

"Yes," agreed Crishell. "It's much better than squealing for a woodcutter to come and save you, like Red Riding Hood."

"It's like you too" said Grace. "You stood up to Russell in the end."

"Do you think so?" said Crishell. "I think I squealed for a woodcutter and you and the others came to help."

Grace gave her a hug. She was never going to understand why Crishell was so nice to Russell, but it didn't matter, as long as she was nice to Grace too.

"But there still isn't a story about a girl being nice to her half brother or sister," said Grace. "It's beginning to look as if I'll have to write my own."

"I'll help you," said Crishell. "We make a good writing team."

That night, when Nana went home, Ma said, "Grace, we got a huge phone bill this morning. What's this expensive call to The Gambia all about? I haven't called your Papa recently."

"Well, maybe you should have," said Grace.

"Now, Grace," said Vince gently. "Don't be cheeky to your ma."

"I wasn't," said Grace. "But he didn't know about the baby and I really needed to talk to him."

"I think we should let it go this time, Ava," said Vince. "But, Grace, can you ask me before making any more long-distance calls? Or maybe you could e-mail your dad? He does have e-mail, doesn't he?"

"Yes," said Grace. "Though it's not the same as talking to someone, is it?" Still, she knew that Ma and Vince could have been a lot crosser with her. She looked at the bill and saw how much her call had cost. "I'm sorry," she said.

Vince went to make them all one of his special smoothies to cheer them up.

"Are you OK about the new baby, Grace?" asked Ma. "You would tell me if you weren't, wouldn't you?"

And she looked so tired and anxious that Grace said, "Of course, I'm fine about the baby. I'm looking forward to it."

And she really, really wanted that to be true.

"Let me show you something," said Ma. And she took Grace up to her bedroom.

In her jewelry box lay her old wedding ring—the one that Papa had given her.

"You do still have it," said Grace.

"Of course," said Ma. "I loved your Papa. In fact, in a way, I still do. I have some happy memories of our time together. But I love Vince too. Sometimes you just have to let the past be the past and live for the present."

"It's a bit like me and Aimee and Crishell, isn't it?" said Grace. "Aimee's still the best friend I ever had, but now that she's gone away, Crishell is the person I want to spend the most time with."

"But it's different with the new baby," said Ma, "because I still have my old baby."

And she gave Grace a hug.

Bravo, Grace!

Sometimes Grace thought that her Ma was not very keen on the new baby idea herself. Ma wasn't getting any bigger; in fact, she had lost weight. She was very sick in the mornings and often looked terrible when she drove off to work with Vince.

"It'll pass," said Nana, when Grace asked her about it. "It's always worst in the first three months."

"Was she like that with me?" asked Grace.

"Just the same," said Nana.

Good, thought Grace. Maybe that means it'll be a girl.

It was true that by the end of the term, Ma was looking a lot better and was a lot more interested in food. Vince made it his mission to feed her up. Like the witch and Hansel, thought Grace.

In the last week of term, Ms. Woollacott's class was giving three assemblies—Monday,

Wednesday and Friday—for the little kids. *Hansel and Gretel* was a huge success on Monday, with all the little ones calling out "mmm!" as soon as they saw the gingerbread house.

"It's funny how all our fairy tales are about eating," said Grace, who hadn't noticed it before. "Hansel and Gretel eat the house, the wolf eats Little Red Riding Hood and the Beast says he's going to eat Beauty, even though he doesn't."

"And there's all that food laid out for the father," added Maria, who had been brilliant with the props for that scene.

"That's why little kids like them," said Raj. "They're always thinking about food."

"Not just little kids," said Kester. And Crishell nodded. She was looking a lot less thin, because the counseling had been helping her mother to get over her obsession about weight.

Everyone's putting on weight, thought Grace, when she looked at Ma that evening. If she stared really closely, she could see the beginning of a bulge below Ma's waistband.

My sister or brother's in there, thought

Grace, trying it out. But it was no good. It was too weird.

"A penny for them, Grace," Ma said suddenly, and Grace realized that she had been really silent all evening.

"I was thinking about the new baby," she said.

"That's good," said Vince. "We've been thinking about it too."

"Probably a bit too much," said Ma. "You see, Grace, it was a bit of a shock to us."

"We wanted to have more children eventually," said Vince. "But neither of us thought it would be that soon. So we were a bit gobsmacked."

"Me too," said Grace, but she wasn't really listening anymore. Had Vince actually said "more children"? Did that mean he thought of her as his child?

"I mean," Ma was saying, "we hadn't had a chance to talk to you about it, get you used to the idea."

"Or ourselves," added Vince. "I'm not even used to the idea of being married yet— let alone being a dad!"

"You'll be a great dad," said Grace, without thinking. Then she realized it was true. She hadn't liked Vince when he first came into their lives, because he was so big and noticeable and always somehow *there*, taking up Ma's time and attention. But now a series of pictures came into her head—Vince helping to rescue Crishell when she fell through the ice on the pond last winter, Vince giving Grace a cell phone for Christmas so that she could talk to Aimee, Vince fixing the gate between the two gardens, Vince giving her the amethyst earrings, Vince cooking breakfast in Nana's flowery apron, Vince making sure she got into the wedding car with him and Ma . . .

Now she realized that she liked the bigness of him; it made him feel permanent and reliable. And the fact that he was always there was a good thing. A good thing in a dad, anyway. Her own papa was hundreds of miles away.

It took only a few seconds to think all these things, because Vince was still making her a little bow and saying, "Why, thank you, Grace," when she realized her eyes were filling up with tears, and she had to run out of the room.

"Leave her, Vince," said Ma quietly. "She'll be fine."

But Grace didn't feel fine. How could she be so disloyal to her own papa? It was like going to The Gambia all over again, when she had seen Papa and Jatou and their two children as a complete family without her. First she had felt left out and jealous and then, when she had started to like Jatou, she had felt guilty because it felt unfair to Ma.

But this was going to be much harder because, as Nana had said, she was going to be living all the time with Ma and Vince and the new baby. And then they would be a family of four—two parents and two children—just like the family in her old school reading book. And people would see them out together and think that Vince was Grace's father too. And Papa would be the odd one out.

She was longing to talk to Nana about it,

and started to tell her about it as soon as they got in the car to go to school next morning. Nana let Grace pour out all her feelings. She was a good listener.

"Well, honey," she said, when Grace had talked herself to a standstill, "You've done a lot of thinking about all this. I've been thinking a bit about it too. It seems to me as if families are all shapes and sizes nowadays. And, what's more, they keep on changing. It's the same for everyone. Take me, for instance. When I was a little girl, there was me and my brother . . ."

"Great-uncle Maxie," said Grace.

"Exactly, only he wasn't anybody's great-uncle then. He was just a skinny little kid," said Nana. "Well, there was us and our Ma and Papa. Then we grew up and I married your Grandpa and Maxie married Carmel. And then my family was me and your Grandpa and our little girl Ava."

"That was Ma," said Grace. They were parked outside the school now but there was still five minutes before the bell. "And then she grew up and married my Papa."

"Yes, she married Antony and they had you

and that was your family for a while, just the three of you."

"And then Papa left us and Grandpa died and you came to live with us," said Grace. "Only I don't remember, because I was very small."

"And then it was the three of us," said Nana.

"For ages," said Grace. "I thought it would be forever."

"Well, now you know that isn't so," said Nana.

"And Papa said he wanted one family, not two, when we went to visit him, do you remember?"

"I do," said Nana. "And I was proud of you, the way you took to your new little sister and brother. And I'm sure I'll be proud of you again when the new baby comes."

"Aren't you proud of me now, Nana?" asked Grace.

"Of course I am, child, but I'll be even prouder if you get yourself into school on time," said Nana, as the bell started to clang.

Little Red Riding Hood was a great success with the little ones on Wednesday. They booed at Kester the wolf and cheered when the woodcutter came on. They specially liked the bit where Sally popped up from under Kester's nightie. So did Crishell. When Kester took his bow at the end, she turned to Grace and said, "Isn't he wonderful?" then looked very embarrassed.

And then, Crishell went up to Kester and gave him a big kiss and it was his turn to be embarrassed. But Grace saw that he kissed her back.

She couldn't wait to tell Nana. When she got into the car after school, she was full of it.

"What big eyes you have, Grace!" said Nana.

"That's what the little girl is supposed to say to the grandmother," said Grace, "not the other way around. Guess what?"

"What?" said Nana obediently.

"It isn't Russell who is Crishell's boyfriend," said Grace. "It's Kester!"

"Well, if that doesn't beat all!" said Nana.

That night, Ma told Grace she had been

given a special test at the hospital and that she and Vince now knew the sex of the baby.

"Do you want to know too, Grace?" she asked. "It is entirely up to you."

Grace thought about it. "No," she said at last. "I think I'd prefer it to be a surprise."

Ma and Vince exchanged looks. Even Vince knew already how much Grace hated surprises and liked to be prepared.

"Are you sure?" he said.

Grace nodded.

Parents weren't allowed at the special assemblies, so no one saw the three plays except the teachers and the little kids. After *Beauty and the Beast*, Grace and her gang all felt a bit flat, even though it was the last day of school and the summer holidays stretched invitingly ahead.

"We should do them again," said Kester.

"Yeah," said Raj. "Let's do them at Grace's and invite our families. I bet we know all the words by heart and the five of us can play all the parts."

So they spent the rest of the afternoon collecting props and asking Ms. Woollacott if they could take things home.

Then Grace had an idea. "Suppose we did the story I wrote for the baby as a fourth play."

"OK," said Crishell. "I'm sure we could turn it into a play—it's just like a fairy tale."

For the next week the whole gang rehearsed, including Maria, who didn't mind being Red Riding Hood and Beauty now that there were only her friends and family to see her. Grace and Crishell made real programs and all the gang's parents were invited.

They had never had such good costumes and props for any of their shows, what with the things they had brought from school and the contents of Grace's dress-up box, which still lived in the old apartment. It now held lots of lace shawls and straw hats and dangly black jet jewelry that used to belong to Mrs. Myerson.

On the day of the performance, all the grown-ups gathered in Grace's old garden and Grace opened the gate to usher them into chairs on the lawn of the house.

"Presenting . . ." said Kester in a loud voice, "*Hansel and Gretel, Little Red Riding Hood, Beauty and theßast* and *A Tale of Two Halves*!"

The audience loved all the well-known stories, especially when Grace got pushed in the oven by Crishell (I knew it would be fun to be a witch again, Grace thought), Kester and Maria sharing one of Nana's nighties (which was smaller than Tasha's mom's) and Maria kissing a beastly sleeping Raj.

Then it was time for *A Tale of Two Halves*.

"Once upon a time," began Maria. "There were a King and a Queen who had just one daughter . . ."

Crishell and Raj came on with one of Grace's dolls. At first they acted lovey-dovey and then they pretended to quarrel.

"Then the King went away to a new country and was King there, with a new Queen," said Maria. "And the first Queen looked after the baby by herself. It grew into a very clever girl."

Now Grace was the daughter and Kester came on as a new King for Crishell to marry. They gave each other very soppy looks.

"Soon the Queen and the King had

a new baby," said Maria. And the doll was brought back on. Grace cuddled it.

"Oh, my lovely baby sister," she said.

Then Raj came back on with the Beast head Maria had made.

"One day a fearsome beast came and kidnapped the baby," said Maria. And Raj snatched up the doll, roaring terribly and rushing off, while Grace acted being surprised and horrified. Then Crishell and Kester did lots of moaning and wringing of their hands.

"Don't worry," said Grace. "I'll save the baby." She took up a wooden sword that Maria passed to her and set off in pursuit of Raj.

"Rraar!" went Raj. "There's nothing I like better than a nice breakfast of baby!" He pretended to put the doll in his mouth. Then Grace rushed on with the sword and pretended to chop off his head. She held up the cardboard head to show the audience, then carried it off to Crishell and Kester, with the doll under her arm.

"Oh, my precious baby!" said Crishell dramatically. "Oh, my clever daughter!"

Now Raj was narrator. "When the baby

grew up," he said, as Maria came on in a little short dress that used to be Grace's, "she never forgot how her big sister saved her life. And they were the best of friends."

Grace and Maria skipped off together while Raj held up a sign saying THE END. And everyone applauded loudly.

"Bravo, Grace!" said Vince loudly, clapping his hands.

"What does that mean, Ma?" said Grace when everyone had gone home. "Bravo, I mean."

"It means," said Ma, "very well done."

"Ah," said Grace. "Bravo, Ma, then."

"What for?" asked Ma.

"For finding Vince," said Grace. "And, you know, having the baby. I've made up my mind. I really am going to try to be the best sister in the world."

"Then I'm sure you will be," said Ma, giving her a big hug.

"Yes," said Nana. "We all know what it's like when Grace puts her mind to something."

One More Present

———

It was Christmas again and Nana and Vince were cooking the dinner. Ma was taking it easy on the sofa because she was so big; she was already on maternity leave and the baby was due in two weeks.

"Phew," she said, fanning herself with a napkin. "Is the heating on really high?" Ma was always too hot these days.

Grace was running between the kitchen and the living room, doing errands for whichever grown-up needed her.

"Sit down a bit," said Ma. "How's dinner coming along?"

"Great," said Grace. "I think Vince is really getting to be a good cook."

"Remember last year," said Ma, "when Nana forgot to put the turkey in?"

They both laughed. "That was because Vince asked you to marry him," said Grace, "and she was all flustered."

Ma sighed. "So much has happened this year, hasn't it? First the new house, then the wedding and soon the baby. I wouldn't have believed it a year ago."

"And Aimee is gone," said Grace, "but Crishell's much happier. And she and Kester like each other. And Russell's stopped bullying people."

"Grace," called Vince, "can you take the potatoes out?"

"Oh good." said Ma. "It sounds as if we're going to eat."

<hr />

That evening, when they were all playing Monopoly, Ma suddenly winced.

"What is it?" asked Grace.

"A bit too much Christmas pudding, I think," said Ma, shakily. "Will you take over my turn? I'm going to lie down for a bit."

Grace went to kiss her ma goodnight before she went to bed but Ma seemed to be asleep. Nana was staying the night, so Paw-Paw came to sleep on Grace's feet.

In the middle of the night, Grace woke up.

There were strange sounds. She went to her bedroom door and saw Vince, fully dressed, carrying a suitcase. For one awful moment, in her sleepy state, Grace thought he was going to leave them.

"Don't go, Vince!" she said, flinging her arms round him.

Vince gave her a big grin. "I've got to go, Grace. Your ma's about to make me a dad and I need to be there."

"You're a dad already, remember?" said Grace, giving him a hug. "My stepdad."

Ma came out of the bedroom, looking a bit wobbly. "Oh, Grace," she said. "I'm so glad you're awake. It looks as if you're going to be a big sister earlier than we thought."

Nana came up the stairs with her hair in curlers, carrying a mug. "Oh, are you off?" she said. "What about your tea?"

"Too late for that," said Ma, trying to smile. "If Vince doesn't take me soon, this baby's going to be born on the stairs!"

"You drink it, Nana," said Grace, when the others had gone. The house seemed very still and quiet after all the rushing about.

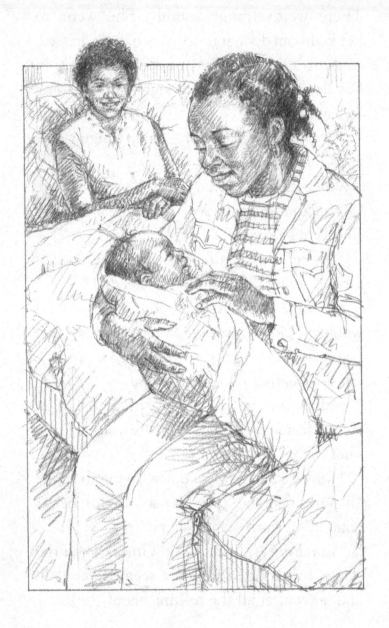

Nana sat down on the stairs and pulled Grace inside her big warm dressing gown. They shared the mug of tea and waited for Vince's phone call.

———∞∞∞———

"A boy!" said Crishell, when Grace phoned her next morning.

"Benjamin Jack," said Grace. "Ma and Vince had the name Benjamin all ready, but I chose Jack, because he was born on Boxing Day—Jack-in-the-Box!"

"Have you seen him yet?" asked Crishell.

"We're just off to the hospital," said Grace. She was feeling quite light-headed from lack of sleep.

"How does it feel to be a sister?" asked Crishell.

"Great," said Grace. "I think."

Later, she held her baby brother in her arms for the first time.

"Hello, Ben," she said.

Ma seemed tired but happy. Vince looked as if he would never stop smiling. He was holding a video camera.

"What do you think of him?" Ma said.

"He's perfect," said Grace. And it was true. "I don't want him to be my half brother," she said suddenly. "I want all of him to be my brother."

"Bravo, Grace," said Nana softly.